This book belongs to:

....

....

Mr Mumbles' Magic Feast

and other stories

Written by
NICOLA BAXTER

Illustrated by
SASCHA LIPSCOMB

This is a Parragon Book
This edition published in 2002

Parragon
Queen Street House
4 Queen Street
Bath BA1 1HE, UK

ISBN 0-75259-496-6

Produced for Parragon by
Nicola Baxter

Designed by Amanda Hawkes
Cover designed by Gemma Hornsby
Cover illustrated by Andrew Everitt- Stewart

Printed in Italy

Contents

Mr.
Mumbles'
Magic
Feast

Mr. Mumbles was a magician—a very good magician. He didn't do tricks. He did real magic that made his neighbours gasp and feel dizzy. That, to be fair, wasn't completely because they were so astonished by the brilliance of Mr. Mumbles' magic. You see, Mr. Mumbles had a most unfortunate sense of humour. He thought it was hilarious to up-end his friends in a huge vat of banana jelly or hang them by their braces on the weather vane of the village church. It was great to

be in the audience of one of Mr. Mumbles'
Magic Shows, but awful if you happened
to be someone plucked out to take part in
one of the magician's spectacles.

Frankly, it's always a problem when
a person with magic powers thinks he or
she is funny. Ordinary practical jokes
played by ordinary people are bad
enough, but when someone with a sense
of silliness can use magic to make the
daftest idea come true, then everyone has
to look out. Practical *magical* jokes can go
too far.

Mr. Mumbles went too far much
too often. In the time that he had lived in
Spellville, there had been more different
inhabitants of the houses on either side
than most hotels see in a year. It's not
much fun to live in a house and not know
if a tide of purple custard is about to roll
over the fence. Or to wake to find that

every single item in your home has been turned upside down in the night.

One poor family moved house so quickly that their eldest son was *still* a parrot when they left—and probably still is to this day.

Of course, some brave souls have tried to tackle Mr. Mumbles on the subject. He's not a malicious man. He only means to have fun. It's just that Mr. Mumbles' idea of fun included turning dogs into hippopotamuses.

The first person to try to get Mr. Mumbles to see the error of his ways was old Lady Lollipop. She was a rich and powerful person in the town, who was appalled when she found that her long-serving (and long-suffering!) maid had been turned into a penguin. (Well, she always wore black and white and she waddled, so Mr. Mumbles didn't think it would make much of a difference. Penguins, however, are appallingly bad at carrying trays of early-morning tea!)

Lady Lollipop marched straight down to see Mr. Mumbles, all too conscious that she had had to put on her own hat (penguins are not too nifty at that either) and wasn't very good at such technical operations.

Mr. Mumbles was sitting in his garden, perfecting a spell to turn wedding cakes into armadillos. It was unfortunate, perhaps, that Lady Lollipop's hat looked quite so much like a wedding cake or that she had a life-long allergy to armadillos. The lady came out in blue spots and ran home screaming, the armadillo clinging to her head every step of the way. The only good thing to come out of all this was that the penguin and the armadillo became great friends and were often to be seen trotting down the road, hand in hand, on a summer's afternoon.

Mr. Blenkins at the bank was the next person to try to bring Mr. Mumbles to heel. He nearly had a heart attack when the magician came in one day and suggested (only half as a joke) that it would be an easy matter to change all the banknotes in the place into birthday cards.

"What for?" gasped Mr. Blenkins, trying to come to terms with the enormity of the catastrophe Mr. Mumbles was suggesting—and failing completely. He felt ill just about where his breakfast was sitting minding its own business.

"Oh, just for fun, you know!" laughed Mr. Mumbles. "I could turn them all back again in an instant—probably!"

Mr. Blenkins found himself as near to begging as a bank manager is ever likely to get. He offered Mr. Mumbles special terms on his account in return for a total lack of magic inside the bank. Mr. Mumbles, delighted at the effect he was having, accepted the deal.

It's a pity that Mr. Blenkins didn't consider the small print of the agreement as closely as he always advised his clients to do. Mr. Mumbles kept to his word. He didn't do a thing *inside* the bank. But when Mr. Blenkins arrived at work the next morning, he was appalled to see that the words "Spellville Central Bank", three feet high above the bank's massive doors, had mysteriously become "Smellville Central Bank".

Mr. Blenkins took the precaution of visiting Mr. Mumbles at the magician's home. He didn't want to tempt the spellmaker by showing him the inside of the bank again.

"Look here," said Mr. Blenkins, "this can't go on, you know. Some of the townsfolk are frightened to go out of their houses in case you turn them into ostriches or put raccoons on their heads.

"I have never, in my whole magical career, turned someone into an ostrich or put a raccoon on her head," said Mr. Mumbles loftily and, in fact, truthfully.

"I'm talking about the principle of the thing," replied Mr. Blenkins through clenched teeth. "Poor Lady Lollipop has retired to the coast to get over her ordeal. She thought it would be more comfortable for her pen... for her maid as well. That means she is no longer using the bank, Mr. Mumbles. It's not good for business at all."

Mr. Mumbles simply laughed.

"I promise you, Mr. Blenkins," he said, "that I will never ever turn you into a penguin or put an armadillo on your head. How's that? I'm a man of my word, you know."

Mr. Blenkins knew exactly what this meant and was not deceived.

"I would simply like to suggest that you confine your magic to entertainment," he said. The whole town loves your shows. It's just when they make people uncomfortable that you lose fans. What if you just used your considerable talents for amusing us all?"

"Well, all the things I do amuse *me*," replied Mr. Mumbles, "and I'm sorry that so few of my neighbours are able to take a joke. However, I can see that you think there is bad feeling in the town, and I don't want that. I'll give it some thought."

Mr. Mumbles put on his thinking cap, which was old and home to several spiders and a small bird, and did some serious ... well, thinking. He didn't want everyone to dislike him, even if he did consider they were making a big fuss about nothing. What could he do to put things right? Suddenly, Mr. Mumbles had a Big Idea. The bird flew up in alarm and even the spiders scuttled into his ears for shelter. When Mr. Mumbles had a Big Idea, the thinking hat got very hot.

A week later, every person in Spellville found a purple envelope in his or her mail. Inside was a gilt-edged card on which an exciting invitation was printed.

Mr Mumbles

Magician Extraordinaire

invites you to his

MAGIC FEAST

on Thursday, 10th September at noon.

The date was two weeks away. For the next thirteen days, Mr. Mumbles' Feast was the *only* subject on everyone's lips in Spellville. And the big question that old ladies were asking their maids, young ladies were asking their boyfriends, and little boys were asking their dogs was:

"Are you going?"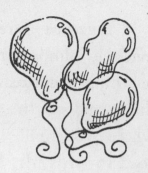
Because, let's face it,
anything to do with
Mr. Mumbles is a
risky business at the
best of times.

"What if he's planning to tie us to
balloons and let us float away?" asked one
stout matron who would have needed a
balloon the size of a house to get her off
the ground. Her friends were kind enough
not to point this out.

"What if the food is magic and
makes us all start talking Chinese?" asked
a little girl. Her mother crisply pointed
out that as long as *everyone* was talking
Chinese, it wouldn't matter in the least.

"Is it safe to take the baby?" an
anxious woman asked her husband.

"Is it safe to take *me*?" he replied.
"That's what I wonder."

Everyone had doubts. Everyone *said* they almost certainly would not go, but human curiosity is a very powerful thing, and on the day of the Feast, the whole of Spellville was trooping down the road towards Mr. Mumbles' house in its very best clothes.

Meanwhile, Mr. Mumbles was relaxing by his swimming pool, aware that several hundred people were about to descend on him, but not in any kind of pre-party tizz.

"That," he said to himself, "is the beauty of magic. It doesn't take any time at all. In fact, almost before you've thought of a spell, it has happened."

As the sound of excited chatter and clomping feet grew nearer and nearer to Mr. Mumbles' gate, the magician stood up at last and waved his hands vaguely in the direction of the house. *Poof piff paff!*

At once a hundred balloons bobbed into the sky, attached to trees, fences and arches. Flags waved gaily from open windows, while on the grass, long trestle tables, groaning with goodies, appeared in a flash. There were silken cushions under the trees, benches and easy chairs for the older folk to sit on, a bouncy castle for the children and penguins everywhere.

Yes, penguins. Mr. Mumbles couldn't help trying to have a joke.

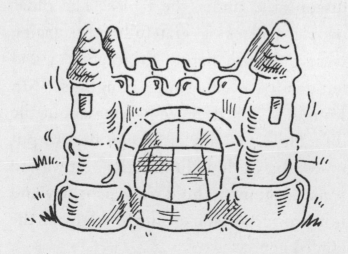

The people of Spellville, crowding through the gate, oohed and aahed at the pretty sight that met their eyes. Some of the children, fed up with having to wear their best and most uncomfortable clothes, dived straight for the buns and disappeared under the tables. The older people, collapsing gratefully into chairs, were only too happy to accept tea and lemonade—even from penguins. Mr. Mumbles smiled. Since hearing about the difficulties of Lady Lollipop, he had put quite a bit of thought into the best way to train penguins to hold trays properly and not drop iced fancies into the laps of the landed gentry.

Half an hour passed. An hour passed. Everyone was having a lovely time. Mr. Mumbles passed among his guests, shaking hands and being as polite as he knew how. Very, very gradually, the visitors relaxed. Nothing horrible had happened yet. Maybe they had been wrong about Mr. Mumbles after all. He wasn't such a bad chap. And Lady Lollipop very often did make a fuss about nothing. These penguins were fun! Every home should have one!

By three o'clock, some of the older guests were dozing in the shade. The youngsters were playing a huge game of chase on the vast lawns. The penguins

were making sure that everything was kept clean and tidy and that full plates of cakes, sandwiches and sausage rolls kept coming to replace the empty ones. A polar bear was carrying around a large tray with ice creams and iced lollies. A small band struck up, with an orang-utan on violin, a sheep on drums and a most elegant parrot singing suitable summer songs.

Yes, everything was lovely. The Feast was a tremendous success. Even Mr. Blenkins the bank manager began to feel at ease.

But Mr. Mumbles was, frankly, bored. And I can't tell you how dangerous a bored magician can be. You simply never, ever want to be anywhere near a magician who has time on his hands and—as in the case of Mr. Mumbles—an unreliable sense of humour.

It was the penguins who gave Mr. Mumbles the idea. Very, very slowly, the visitors began to reach for their cardigans and cuddle into their coats as the temperature very, very slowly dropped. There didn't seem to be any reason for it. The sun was shining as brightly as ever and there was no breeze.

Mr. Mumbles rubbed his hands with glee (and to keep them warm) as one by one the visitors stood up and started walking around to keep warm. Much to everyone's astonishment, the swimming pool and the lake began to ice over. Before they could gather their wits, the guests were astonished to see six penguins and the polar bear giving a virtuoso skating display on the swimming pool.

Mr. Mumbles was charm itself.

"I can't imagine what is happening to the weather," he said, handing around blankets to those whose noses looked bluest or who were shivering so much they could not applaud the skating.

Only Mr. Blenkins had the presence of mind to think coldly (it was, in fact, impossible to think in any other way!) about the situation. The more he thought about it, the more certain he was that Mr. Mumbles was responsible for the big freeze. He hurried off to find his host.

Mr. Mumbles was just wondering whether to make it snow when Mr. Blenkins found him. The bank manager was a clever man but a logical one. The whole business of magic made him anxious and apprehensive. But as he saw Mr. Mumbles standing there, he suddenly realized that this was not a problem about magic. This was a problem about a bored and lonely man. If Mr. Mumbles had not been a magician, he would have been the kind of person to put plastic poached eggs on your plate and plastic spiders in your cereal. Because he had magical powers, his jokes were more extreme, that was all.

So as Mr. Blenkins shivered his way towards Mr. Mumbles, he didn't prepare an angry speech or fall on his knees and beg for better weather. Instead, he laughed … as heartily as he could manage with his teeth chattering.

"Ho ho ho! Ha ha ha! Well done, Mumbles!" he chortled.

Mr. Mumbles turned towards him with a look of such amazed delight on his face that Mr. Blenkins knew he had been right about the man.

"Do you like it?" he asked, like a little boy showing off his new train. "It's funny, isn't it? I got the idea from the penguins, you see."

"It's brilliant!" said Mr. Blenkins warmly (as far as his voice was concerned) and very coldly (as far as the rest of him was concerned), "and I'll tell you what would be even better." He whispered into Mr. Mumbles' ear.

So that is how, on the same afternoon, Spellville experienced sunny summer weather, arctic conditions, and a tropical heatwave that caused a jungle to grow up around the magician's house. When they realized that nothing terrible was going to happen, the guests loved it. Before long, grannies were casting off their cardigans and going swimming in their vests and bloomers.

Mr. Blenkins was a sensible man. Most of the town was a client of his one way or another. Before the week was out, he had explained to everyone how to deal with Mr. Mumbles. All of a sudden, the folk of Spellville could see the advantages of having a magician in their midst instead of the disadvantages. And Mr. Mumbles was delighted to find that he was the most popular person in the place.

Only Lady Lollipop, hearing of events by phone from her seaside stay, had her doubts. But then she also still had an untrained penguin, so perhaps that is understandable!

The Unwilling Warthog

Have you ever looked in the mirror and wished you were someone else? It happens to the best of us on a Monday morning when many of us wake up looking as if we're in dire need of a head transplant. Even supermodels, I'm told, sometimes peer into the glass and say, "Aaaaaaagh!"

Certainly, Wilbur the warthog knew all about those kinds of feelings. He didn't, of course, have a bathroom mirror, but he did have a perfectly good waterhole that reflected his ... er ... *characterful* face early each morning when he went for a drink and a wash. (Yes, it *was* in the same water, but don't let's forget he was a warthog with warthog ways.)

It didn't matter how cheerful Wilbur was feeling after a night of dreams about everything he liked best in the world. When he saw his reflection in the waterhole, he went, "Aaaaaaagh!" as if it was the first time he had ever seen his large, hairy face.

You see, Wilbur didn't want to be a warthog. I know and you know that if you are born a warthog you will be a warthog for the rest of your days, but Wilbur clung to a feeble hope that it was a mistake. He didn't mind the idea of being any other kind of animal. He just didn't like warthogs very much.

When Wilbur was still only a warthoglet, his mother found him one day mincing across the savannah and waggling his nose in the air.

"What on earth are you doing, Wilbur?" she asked. "You'll damage your trotters walking like that. Mincing is not the warthog way."

"I'm not a warthog," Wilbur replied. "I'm a rather short giraffe, but I'll grow one day soon."

Wilbur's mother called his father.

"You need to have a word with that boy," she said. "He seems to think he's a giraffe, as if anyone would want to be one of those useless, lanky lollopers. I'm glad he has ambitions, but he needs to know that there is no way he will ever be a giraffe. And thank goodness for that!"

Wilbur's father did have a word. The word was "Fathead!" and he used it liberally. Poor Wilbur looked stunned and close to tears.

"You mean I'm *never* going to be a giraffe?" he snorted plaintively. "Never ever? But surely, when I grow up…"

"When you grow up, you'll be a fine, big warthog like me," said his father, tossing his tusks proudly. "Now let's stop all this silly nonsense. Think how those giraffes would laugh at you if they knew. They're unbearably uppity as it is."

Wilbur looked in horror at his father. He saw a large animal with a tendency towards tubbiness. Wilbur's dad would have called it muscle, but it looked suspiciously like flab to the hoglet. The senior warthog's face was not, to Wilbur's mind, a thing of beauty. It was wrinkled. It was hairy. It had tusks growing out at odd angles. The eyes were small and a bit red (due to late nights at the waterhole) and the nose was large and sniffly. Wilbur, still a sweet little hoglet, showed all the signs of being a very similar warthog at a later stage in his development. He found the thought unbearable.

"You see, I don't *want* to be a warthog," he told his astonished father.

"I'd much rather be some other kind of animal. One that is graceful or fast or clever. Or all three," he added hopefully.

Wilbur's father was aghast. An aghast warthog is not a pretty sight.

"But warthogs *are* graceful," he snorted, and he trotted smartly around his son to prove his point.

Wilbur, coughing from the dust tossed up by his father's less than fairylike feet, was not impressed.

"Not as graceful as a gazelle," he said sulkily.

"Maybe not, but we are certainly fast," claimed his father. He lowered his warty nose and *charged* at an inoffensive tussock of grass in the distance. More dust

was hurled into the air as the heavy hog thundered across the savannah. A nearby antelope looked up in surprise. Warthogs were not known for their speed.

Wilbur waited until his sprinting father, badly out of breath and making a deeply unattractive sound somewhere between a snort and a wheeze, returned to his side.

"That was good," he said graciously, "but a leopard is a lot faster. And it doesn't make that strangled bagpipe noise."

Wilbur's dad took a minute or two to recover himself.

"That business about leopards being fast is over-rated in my opinion," he said. "They can't keep it up for long, while a fit warthog, perhaps a little younger than myself, can jog along for hour after hour. It's staying power that counts in the end, you know."

Now it was Wilbur's turn to snort.

"Don't say another word, Wilbur!" cried his father. "How you can even suggest that warthogs aren't clever, I don't know. Didn't your aunt Susan invent a method of waterhole wallowing that allowed maximum mud coverage? That's pretty clever, if you ask me."

"Some elephants," said Wilbur, "can remember things that happened *years* ago. Chimpanzees use sticks to dig grubs out of holes. Lionesses can creep ever so quietly though the grass until they are ready to *pounce*! Those things are really clever. And some human beings, you know, can make music come out of little boxes. Now that's what I call clever."

Wilbur's dad pawed the ground with his trotter in vexation.

"You should be proud of being a warthog, son," he said. "Imagine, you could have been born a vulture. Ugh!"

"At least I'd be able to fly," said Wilbur. "And other animals would respect me a bit."

"You call it respect. I'd call it fear and loathing," replied his father. "Surely you'd rather be a warthog than a snake? They don't even have legs!"

"They don't need them," said Wilbur. "They don't have ugly trotters and fat, hairy knees, either."

"It's no use talking to you," grunted the older warthog. "I'm going off for a good wallow."

Later, he took Wilbur's mother on one side.

"Who's been filling the boy's head with this nonsense?" he asked. "There's no finer calling in life than warthoghood. I tried to tell him that, but he wouldn't listen. He's a bit of a loner. Maybe he should spend more time with warthogs his own age. I'll ask my sister and her hoglets to visit. A bit of rough-and-tumble with his cousins will soon sort Wilbur out."

But Wilbur didn't get on at all well with five lively hoglets. He found them rough and rude. After a couple of days, the hoglets refused to even try to play with Wilbur.

"He's weird," they said. "He doesn't like mud and he snorts in a funny way. Let's go home again, Mum."

Wilbur was on his own again. His feelings of disgust at being a warthog didn't change. Mornings when he arrived at the waterhole were a nightmare to him. During his dreams, he could imagine himself a zebra or a lion. The shimmering water destroyed all such illusions. Staring back at him was (to his eyes) a perfectly hideous face, with growing tusks and little hairy ears. Wilbur tried to wash and drink with his eyes shut, but nearly drowned in the process.

Then, one day, a human being in a truck came to the waterhole. He didn't have a box that made music, but he did have a similar box that he kept holding to his face and clicking with. He made a camp near the waterhole and set about clicking at every animal he could find.

For a while, Wilbur watched the human in awe. Although not as graceful as a gazelle or as fast as a leopard, he was pretty clever. He could make a fire and drive a truck (which meant that he didn't *need* to be able to run like a leopard). He could do up buttons with his wiggly fingers, which Wilbur, looking in despair at his own stiff little trotters, envied enormously. The human being could creep, too, very like a lion, when he wanted to click at a fierce animal. He could poke grubs out of a hole with a stick just as well as a chimpanzee. At least, it wasn't exactly a hole. It was a round, shiny thing with pinkish-red grubs inside. They were obviously just as delicious as ordinary white grubs, though, because the human being ate lots of them.

Wilbur longed more than anything else to be a human being. He thought the camper was wonderful. But being a human being, he discovered, wasn't easy.

Wilbur tried sitting crosslegged, as the human did in front of his fire, and had to call for help to get his legs untangled. Wilbur tried to drive the camper's truck when he wasn't looking, and almost frightened the life out of himself when he put his trotter firmly on the horn. Finally, Wilbur tried to click with one of the human's clicking things, but although he touched it very delicately with the tips of his trotters, it made a horrible crunching sound and didn't really look the same shape afterwards. The human being made a lot of vulture-type noises and hopped up and down on the spot when he found the squashed clicker. Wilbur wondered if this marvellous creature could actually fly, but the human simply got very red in the face and had to sit down to recover. Wilbur, who had never seen a human child, wondered if perhaps the creature was still

young and hadn't yet learnt to take off.
He still thought the camper was the most
amazing animal he had ever seen.

Wilbur's mother and father tried
hard to talk him out of his adoration of
the human being.

"You can't trust them," said his
father. "One minute they're going, 'Oooh,
aaaah! Look at the lovely animals!' The
next they're trying to catch you in a net
or," he added darkly, "worse."

Wilbur would hear none of it. Even when his mother told him she had heard a rumour that humans ate something called pigs, animals with snouts and trotters not unlike his own, Wilbur would not be put off. He went to sleep each night (stretched out uncomfortably in an unwarthoglike but faintly human way) wishing with all his heart that he could wake up and find that he had wiggly fingers and a tiny head.

All this time, the human had been clicking at elephants and zebras, antelopes and gazelles. He had crept through the grass to click at a lion sleeping in the sun and stood very still for hours on end until a couple of snooty giraffes deigned to drift in his direction.

Suddenly, one sunny morning, the human started clicking at warthogs.

"I don't like this," said Wilbur's father. "Come on, Mavis, we're getting out of here. Wilbur! Follow us! Ready? Quick waddle!"

But Wilbur, fascinated by his hero's activities, didn't move a muscle. And with his father, mother and various neighbours gone, he suddenly became the centre of attraction himself. The human was clicking furiously. Wilbur did his best to strike interesting poses. Somehow, they didn't make the human happy. He wanted pictures of *warthogs*, not animals that looked on the surface like warthogs but appeared to act like supermodels.

The more Wilbur posed, the more exasperated the human being appeared to become. He crept closer and closer, hoping, perhaps, to be able to click at Wilbur's face and avoid his waving trotters. Wilbur, still posing like mad, retreated to the muddiest part of the waterhole. The human advanced.

Now Wilbur could have told the human being quite a lot about how to negotiate the terribly muddy mud at the edge of the waterhole, but he was too busy posing even to snort in alarm. There was a sudden cry of, "*Ooooooooeeerr*!" and a enormous *SPLASH*! Suddenly the waterhole was full of a wallowing warthog, a spluttering human and a couple of curious crocodiles, who had slithered off the bank to see what all the fuss was about.

Wilbur wondered the same thing. The human being was making an incredible amount of noise and splashing, splattering Wilbur and the crocodiles with mud and water in a way they rather enjoyed.

It was a while before Wilbur realized that the human was in distress. It was several moments longer before his brain could take in the awful truth—this human could not swim!

A warthog's mind does not work particularly quickly. By the time Wilbur decided he must take some action, the human had managed to find some mud under his feet and begun to stagger to the edge of the waterhole. It was then that he saw the crocodiles...

Now Wilbur had the sense to know that a young and frisky crocodile can be less than friendly, but to be afraid of old Gladys and Fred seemed ridiculous. All of a sudden, Wilbur saw the human with new eyes. He simply looked silly.

I won't say that Wilbur became proud of his warthogishness overnight, but from that day he did see himself in a different light. It wasn't long before he found he could think of something to despise about every creature—not just humans. And this, although not a very pleasant characteristic, is typical of warthogs the world over. At last, Wilbur was an unwilling warthog no longer.

Carol
and the
Contest Car

Each morning when she woke up, Carol looked out of the window to make sure her car was still there. It's the kind of thing a lot of people do, especially in areas where things have to be chained down to stay in one place for more than an hour or two, but it's not so usual for someone of Carol's age to *have* a car. She was eight years and two months old. And it really was her car. She had won it in a competition at the supermarket.

It was a bright Saturday morning when Carol and her mother went shopping. The supermarket was packed, as usual.

"This is hopeless," said Carol's mum, looking at the queues. "Let's go and raid the café."

Although the rest of the shop was heaving with people, the café was usually very quiet. That was because the coffee was disgusting and the sandwiches looked as if they had died in the night. But Carol and her mother weren't worried about coffee or sandwiches. For some reason, the café served the best chocolate cake either of them had ever tasted. They ate it with lemonade and it was a real treat. So far, only a few other people seemed to have discovered it.

The lady behind the counter greeted Carol and her mother like old friends.

"The usual?" she asked, but she didn't even wait for a reply. She was already cutting big wedges of cake and dumping it unceremoniously on to thick white plates.

Carol and her mother didn't mind that the cake looked as though it had been through a mincer before they even tasted it. It was, after all, the taste that was heavenly.

"Mmmmmmm," said Carol.

"Mmm mmm *mmmm*," replied her mother. "This is what makes shopping bearable. Mmmm."

The lady from behind the counter was passing their table, wiping up crumbs from other tables in a way that only made them look worse. She laughed when she heard what Mrs. Ferguson was saying.

"It wouldn't be half as bad, dear, if you won that car," she said. "It's trudging home with the shopping that takes it out of you, in my opinion."

Mrs. Ferguson privately thought that the whole experience (except the cake) took it out of her, but she asked, "What car?" all the same.

"Oh, there's a lovely new car to be won in aisle five," said the lady. "All you have to do is to guess how many cornflakes there are in a box."

"Couldn't you just buy some and see how many were usually in the box?" asked Carol's mother.

"Oh no, dear!" laughed the woman. "It's a huge box. It's bigger than your little one here. That's why it's hard. Mind you, there have been students from the university here all week taking all sorts of measurements and doing calculations on their computers. They reckon they can work it out what they call scientifically."

"Hmmm, it doesn't sound as if we stand much of a chance then," said Mrs. Ferguson, eating the last crumbs of her chocolate cake.

"It's still worth a go, though," said the café lady. "You only have to buy one box of cornflakes to try. And after all, you'd probably be doing that anyway."

"Mum," said Carol, as they brushed the chocolate crumbs from their laps and went back to the entrance to find a trolley, "you won't do anything *silly*, will you?"

Mrs. Ferguson snorted.

"Whatever give you that idea?" she demanded. "Silly, indeed!"

Carol mentioned gherkins, sardines and toothpaste, of which the household still had big enough supplies to last until they were all in their nineties, including Carol.

"That was different," said her mother. "There was a real chance of winning with those competitions, and why we didn't, I can't imagine. I'm sure

all these contests are rigged, you know. I've got absolutely no intention of buying cornflakes we don't want and don't need in order to enter a competition we don't stand a chance of winning."

But when the pair, steering their trolley at dangerous speed along the aisles, suddenly came around the corner into aisle five and saw the car, they stopped dead in their tracks.

"Oh," said Carol's mother.

"Ah," said Carol.

There was something about that car. It gleamed under the shop lights. Its slinky headlights shone and its windows twinkled. It was a shiny silver colour, with a red stripe down the side. Silver and red were Carol's favourite colours. And best of all was its number plate: CF1.

Carol looked at her mother. Her mother looked back.

"How many boxes of cornflakes could we eat in a year?" asked Carol.

"Loads," said her mother, and began to pull some off the shelf. The trolley was soon full.

"We've got sixty-four boxes," Mrs. Ferguson told the assistant standing near an enormous box of cornflakes. "Where do I make my guesses?"

Mrs. Ferguson sat down at the table provided with a sheaf of entry forms. It took her ages and ages to fill them all in.

"Four million, seven hundred thousand and three," she wrote on the first form. "Nine hundred and forty-eight thousand and seventy- two," she wrote on the second. Carol sighed. It was clear that her mother had not the faintest idea how many cornflakes could possibly be in the box. The likelihood of her winning seemed very small indeed.

After what seemed like ages, Mrs. Ferguson stopped writing and shook her wrists vigorously.

"It makes your arm ache, writing so fast," she said. "It reminds me of exams at school. Well, we've done our best. Now we just have to wait."

She got up to leave with the huge trolleyful of boxes, but the assistant called her back and pointed to the floor under the table.

"You dropped one," she said. "You might as well have all your goes."

"Oh, I couldn't write another one," said Mrs. Ferguson. "You do it, Carol."

Carol screwed up her eyes. Then she wrote down the biggest number she could possibly think of. Then she added three noughts for luck, put down her name and address, and helped her mother struggle home with the shopping. It involved … er

... *borrowing* the trolley (and to be honest there were already three of those in the back garden from the gherkin, sardine and toothpaste fiascos).

I wish I could say that both Carol and her mother forgot all about the contest in the weeks that followed, but it's hard to forget about cornflakes when your bedroom is piled high with boxes of them and you are eating them for breakfast, lunch and supper.

After a week and a half, Carol hoped she would never see another cornflake in her life. When Christmas came and went, and most of their relatives had been less than enthusiastic about receiving a breakfast product as a present, the pile hardly seemed to have lessened at all. Mrs. Ferguson wondered idly if she could build a conservatory with the boxes. Carol remembered an ill-fated attempt to make modern sculpture with sardine cans and begged her not to try.

It was one day in early February when a letter arrived addressed to Ms. C. Ferguson. Carol's mother opened it, read it and collapsed under the table.

When Carol had revived her by flapping a magazine in her face and sprinkling water over her (well, sloshing would be a more accurate term), Mrs.

Ferguson sat up and reached for the letter. She read it again and gulped.

"I won the car!" she said. "The cornflake car—I won it! No more trudging for us. It'll be whizzing all the way! I can't believe it!"

Carol looked at the letter.

"You shouldn't," she said, "it's not true. Look!"

"I have looked," replied her mother. "I've looked three times. It's perfectly clear. It's on proper headed paper. It's not a hoax or one of our relatives trying to pay us back for the cornflake presents. This is the genuine article. Look, there's a phone number to use. I'm going to ring up and confirm it."

Before Carol could say another word, her mother was on the phone and arranging for delivery. Carol bit her lip. She couldn't decide whether to say anything or not. It seemed a terrible shame to disappoint her mother, who was now dancing some kind of cancan around the kitchen and unfortunately bringing quite a few sardine cans, stashed in odd places, hurtling around her head.

Carol went up to her bedroom and consulted her ancient teddy bear.

"The thing is," she said, "I know it was my ticket that won. I know the

number off by heart and it's on the letter. But Mum hasn't been as happy as this for years. And I can't even drive for another nine years. Should I tell her or not?"

The old bear looked glum.

"I knew you'd say that," said Carol. "Okay, I'll keep quiet."

Carol crept around for the rest of the day, weighed down by her guilty secret. Her mother was on the phone to various of her friends who, over the years, had made cutting remarks about the insane waste of money that entering competitions represented. Mrs. Ferguson was obviously enjoying herself hugely.

The man from the cornflake company arrived bright and early the next morning. He tried to persuade Mrs. Ferguson to allow him to take her picture with the car, but Carol's mother, who had been spreading the word all afternoon and evening the day before, suddenly became coy and refused. As a matter of fact, this was because she hadn't been to the hairdresser for a few weeks and didn't want to appear at less than her best.

"Well," said the cornflake man at last, when he had given up trying to persuade her, "I'll leave you to enjoy your new car. If you can just give me the entry form ticket, I'll be on my way. You did keep it, didn't you?"

"Oh yes, no problem," said Mrs. Ferguson. "I stuck them on the fridge with all my other important papers. Now let me see."

There were sixty-three tickets stuck on to the fridge with magnets in the shape of sardines (consolation prizes in the sardine competition). It took some time for Mrs. Ferguson to work through them all. At last she gave a sigh of satisfaction.

"Here you are," she said. "D798324. That's it."

The man shook his head.

"No, I need D798325," he said.

Mrs. Ferguson began frantically to fan through her tickets again, but Carol, clutching her old bear for moral support, decided it was time to speak up.

"Here it is," she said. "D798325. It's my ticket."

There was an awful silence in the kitchen as Carol's mother gazed at her with a glazed expression.

"But *I'm* Ms. C. Ferguson," she said plaintively.

"So am I," said Carol. "And it is my ticket. There isn't anything to stop me winning the car, is there?"

"No," said the cornflake man, glad now that he hadn't bothered to take lots of photos of Carol's mother. "I can't persuade you to pose for publicity shots, I suppose?" he added.

"No," said Carol. "I'd just like the keys, please."

By the time the man had left, Mrs. Ferguson had recovered a little.

"Well," she said, "I don't suppose it matters very much which one of us has won it. Shall we go for a drive right now? Aren't we lucky?"

But Carol had begun to see possibilities in her car.

"I don't think we need to go anywhere in it today," she said. "I'll think about when we can use it."

Mrs. Ferguson narrowed her eyes.

"I can see the way your mind is working and I don't like it, my girl," she said. "What's to stop me just grabbing the keys and doing what I like?"

"I'll swallow them," said Carol.

"You couldn't! Don't be ridiculous. They're much too big," scoffed her mother, but when Carol opened her mouth wide and dangled the keys over it, she squealed, "No, don't! You'll choke or something!"

"I need to go upstairs and talk to old bear," said Carol, "before I decide what to do."

Mrs. Ferguson knew when she was beaten. She gnashed her teeth and paced up and down while Carol took her time deciding on her strategy.

Carol came downstairs at last. She was carrying a list.

1. No more cornflakes – ever.

2. No more gherkins – ditto.

3. Need I mention sardines?

4. No speeding.

5. No racing.

6. No eating crisps in the car.

Mrs. Ferguson clenched her teeth, stomped up and down a bit—and agreed.

"Sometimes, Carol," she said, "I wonder which of us is the grown-up."

"Or which of us isn't," said Carol.

Princess
Pearl

When King Brian and Queen Madge gave birth to their first child, the whole country held its breath for news. All night long, there was to-ing and fro-ing at the palace. Down the echoing corridors, messages from Dr. Bartfinkle, the famous physician, were relayed from one footman to another.

"More hot water!" came the cry.

"More hot water! More hot water! More hot water!" repeated the footmen in their red uniforms.

As the night wore on, the requests became stranger.

"More magazines!"

"More footballs!"

"More knicker elastic!"

"More cheese!"

There was, in fact, a perfectly good explanation for all these requests, but it doesn't have anything to do with this

story. The next important event as far as the new baby was concerned was a loud yell from the royal bedroom.

"Aaaaaagh!" shouted the Queen in an unqueenly way.

"Aaaaaagh!" shouted the new baby in a babylike way.

"Aaaaaagh!" shouted the first footman in a ridiculous way.

"Aaaaaagh!"

"Aaaaaagh!"

"Aaaaaagh!"

"Aaaaaagh!"

The cry echoed through the palace, until it reached the cook in the palace kitchens. And she, being a wise woman and well able to interpret the oddest orders, burst into tears and said, "It's a princess! God bless her!"

The usual practice, when a royal baby was born, was for the proud father to appear on the balcony in front of the palace and show the precious infant to the gathering crowds below. They, I'm afraid, having been celebrating the birth already for several hours, sometimes shouted out things that were not fit for any royal child's ears. It was often a blushing and anxious king or prince who scuttled back inside with his beautiful bundle.

On this occasion, however, no such appearance was made. Indeed, the door of the Queen's chamber remained shut for days. A thoughtful-looking Dr. Bartfinkle finally emerged, shaking his head.

The crowd waiting outside the palace included several eager newspaper reporters. They surged forward as soon as they saw the shiny black hat of the world-famous doctor.

"Is the baby well, Doctor?" they yelled. "There have been rumours that she is ill in some way."

The doctor shook his head.

"The royal princess is perfectly healthy in every way," he said. "There is nothing to worry about *there*."

The way he said these words strongly implied that there *was* something to worry about somewhere else. Like bloodhounds on the scent, the reporters were determined to find it.

"The Queen? Is she recovering well? Was it a difficult birth?"

"All births require a great deal of skill from a specialist physician," replied Dr. Bartfinkle solemnly (if untruthfully), "but I am happy to say that the Queen is doing very well and was up and about remarkably quickly."

There was a puzzled buzzing from the press pack. Then one of them asked the question they had all been wondering about since the birth.

"Why haven't we seen the baby?"

The doctor paused. His usually suave demeanour left him. His famous hat tilted over one eye. His famous frown intensified. Sweat broke out on his brow.

"I really couldn't say," he said. "No doubt the palace will keep you informed."

He scuttled into his carriage and rattled away, fanning himself with his gloves and shaking his head.

For the next few days, wild rumours and extraordinary speculations swept the kingdom. Some said that the child had been stolen just after birth and was being held to ransom. Others claimed that the Queen's maid had dropped the infant and given her a black eye, with which she could not appear in public. Old people who still believed in magic were sure that the princess had been bewitched.

None of them was right.

Back in the palace, the King had called in his most trusted advisors and sworn them to secrecy. He needed advice and he needed it badly. Finally, after seven long days of council meetings, a royal edict was sent out. All looking glasses in the kingdom were to be destroyed. It had been proved, said the edict, that looking at one's own reflection could have a dreadful effect on one's wellbeing.

Now, like me, no doubt you have had mornings when the sight of your face in the bathroom mirror was enough to send you screaming into a darkened room. But most days, the familiar features that grin back at you from the glass are not so bad. Sometimes they even look pretty good. A sensible person knows that there are good mirrors and bad mirrors, and avoids the latter at all costs. So there was a lot of muttering when the royal edict was made known.

The muttering did not die down. In the end, the famous Dr. Bartfinkle was forced to issue a learned book in which he discussed all the many ways in which poor, unsuspecting people were doing themselves untold damage by looking at their own reflections.

The doctor's reputation meant that at least half the population now took the edict seriously. The other half took the King's Army seriously. This band of military misfits was entrusted with the job of removing all looking glasses from the realm. Since the King's Army was one of

the main reasons the country could boast a very small prison population, most people thought it better not to argue when burly soldiers knocked on their doors. Within a fortnight, all the mirrors in the country had been destroyed.

This simple act had devastating results throughout the kingdom. The sales of lipsticks and eyeliners plummeted. No one wants to appear in public with a mouth spreading from ear to ear or eyes that look as if they belong to a panda. For a brief period, sales of shiny saucepans trebled, until the palace got wise to this and ordered that in future all saucepans and other shiny items must be painted black inside and out.

You have probably guessed by now what was the problem with young Princess Pearl, as she was called. She was ugly—not just ugly in the red and wriggly way that lots of babies are ugly, but ugly in a way that made footmen make faces (which they are trained not to do).

Of course, the King and Queen realized that their daughter was not the picture of perfection they had expected. I mean, all princesses are pretty, aren't they? But they loved their daughter dearly and wanted her life to be as pleasant as possible for her.

"She may grow out of it," said the King, hopefully.

"With that nose?" asked the Queen, not so hopefully.

"Something could surely be done about her eyebrows?" ventured the King.

"But not her eyes," replied his wife. Having spent her life trying to look like every subject's idea of what a queen should be, the Queen knew all too well what miracles make-up and a loyal royal beautician could achieve—and what they could not.

Meanwhile, Princess Pearl grew up to enjoy all the things that princesses usually like. She loved to ride her pony in the park. She liked to swish up and down the corridors in her best silk dresses. She liked to try on her crown. But she didn't grow any prettier.

She wasn't, of course, kept locked up in the palace from the day she was born. The King's subjects soon became all too aware of the Princess's problem, but they were far too loyal to say anything about it in print or to her face.

The most important thing as far as the King and Queen were concerned was that Princess Pearl should not herself know how extraordinarily ugly she was.

"It would destroy her confidence," said the Queen. "That's why the edict about the mirrors was so important. We really cannot have a future queen of this country who hides in her room all day. And that, you mark my words, is what would happen if she ever found out."

As time went by, the likelihood that Pearl would one day become Queen became greater, for the royal couple had no more children. As the Princess approached her eighteenth birthday, the Queen for the first time raised a subject that had been on her mind for years.

"What," she said to the King as they enjoyed a royal picnic one day, "are we going to do about finding her a husband?"

The King's answering sigh showed that his wife was not the only one who had considered this matter over the years. It was a ghastly question.

"Are there any princes with ... er ... poor eyesight?" queried the King.

"What a ridiculous idea!" cried the Queen, but she later admitted that there were not—she had checked.

"Perhaps if we offered some presents—a couple of castles, perhaps, or a lake or two?" suggested the King.

"Our daughter deserves better than that," the Queen replied sharply. "She may not be pretty, but she's a dear, sweet girl. We can't possibly marry her off to some mercenary prince who's only interested in adding another castle to his collection."

"You're right," agreed the King, looking a little ashamed, "it's just that..."

"I know," said the Queen. "Believe, me, I know."

"If she doesn't marry," groaned the King, "you know what it will mean."

The royal couple stared glumly at the distant mountains.

"It will mean Melvin," they said in chorus. "Ugh!"

The Prince Melvin in question was a very distant cousin of the King. He was a particularly objectionable man. After his last visit, before Princess Pearl's birth, when he had offended everyone, caused the footmen to go on strike, asked if he might have fried lizards for breakfast and stalked the royal cat with a toasting fork,

the royal family had decided never to invite him again. He was, however, their nearest living relative, and if Princess Pearl died without having children, he would be the next king.

"It wouldn't be *him*, of course," said the Queen, trying to look on the bright side. "He's our age. It would be one of his children."

"Darling, do you imagine that any of his children, if they take after him and his equally objectionable wife, will be any better?" asked the King. "The whole idea makes me quake in my boots, but I admit that it is very likely to happen. However, we mustn't give up without trying. We should hold a party as is customary for Pearl on her birthday and ... here's a thought ... what if it was a *masked* ball?"

"That's brilliant!" cried the Queen. "At least, it's worth a try."

Preparations for Princess Pearl's Birthday Ball were soon in full swing. Invitations were sent to every eligible prince for hundreds of miles. After some thought, the King and Queen extended the guest-list to quite a lot of eligible dukes, earls and lords as well.

For weeks, the royal cooks planned and baked, the royal gardeners pruned and clipped, the royal maids polished and plumped, and the royal footmen ran up and down the corridors shouting. At last

the ballroom was festooned with flowers, a cake of monstrous proportions was prepared, and Princess Pearl put on her gold and silver dress and the larger-than-usual (because of the nose!) mask that had been made for her by the royal jewellers. As the guests trooped in, the band struck up and the thousand twinkling lights of the chandeliers made a fairytale world.

It was a glorious party. What pleased the King and Queen more than anything was that one young man in particular spent a great deal of time dancing with the Princess and even longer talking with her on the balcony. They seemed to be getting on very well.

"Who is he?" hissed the King to the Queen, as they passed each other in a royal rumba.

"Not a clue!" mouthed the Queen, performing a tricky twizzle.

Later, as midnight drew near, the King and Queen seized the opportunity for a quick consultation.

"The trouble is," said the King, "at midnight, all masks will be removed. What will he do then?"

"As long as he behaves like a gentleman and doesn't faint, scream or throw a tantrum, I shall be happy," said the Queen.

Still, as the clock struck, she held her breath, forgetting even to remove her own mask (which didn't really matter as the royal crown was rather a give-away). All eyes were on the Princess and her partner as they removed their masks.

As the Princess revealed her face at last, there was quite a bit of fainting, screaming and throwing of tantrums in the room, but it didn't come from the young man gazing deeply into Pearl's eyes. It was obvious even to the Princess's worried father that the unknown suitor was already far too much in love to be seeing straight at all.

"Love," said the Queen with feeling, echoing his own thoughts, "is a wonderful thing."

Suddenly, the young man hurried from the room and returned carrying a present wrapped in pink and silver paper with a large pink bow.

"Happy birthday, darling," he said.

While the King went red and made a sort of "Hrrrrummmpph" sound at what he considered was undue familiarity from someone whose name he didn't even know, Princess Pearl was unwrapping her present with eagerness.

It was a beautiful, jewelled … mirror!

The Queen started forward, then froze. The King turned from white to red, then back to white. Everyone else in the room held their breaths. There was an awesome silence as the Princess turned over the mirror. She looked. She made a little face. She glanced up at the young man. "Does it matter?" she asked.

"What?" asked the suitor, gazing at her like a puppy.

"I didn't think so," said the Princess. And—to the consternation of the King—she kissed her young man right there in the ballroom.

There was a storm of clapping from the assembled party. The Queen sighed and burst into tears. The King strode forward to find out who exactly he was about to have as a future son-in-law.

"May I have the honour to present myself, Your Highness," said the young man, bowing satisfactorily low, "as Prince James, son of Prince Melvin, your distant cousin, and, if I may be so bold, a suitor for your daughter's hand."

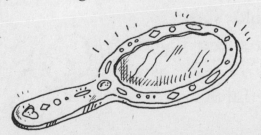

It was almost unbelievable that the objectionable Melvin could have so fine a son. Prince James was tactful, but the royal couple gathered that being brought up by such an unpleasant man had made the Prince value the inside of a person far beyond their outer appearance. He was a perfect match for Princess Pearl.

As for Pearl herself, many people wondered why she had not screamed at the very first sight of herself. What they had not considered is that when you look deeply into another person's eyes, what you see is ... yourself. Pearl had already had several long minutes to view her formidable features in the Prince's eyes and to decide that if he liked them, then she could too.

As the Queen said, love really is a wonderful thing.

Don't Jump, Jiggles!

An ostrich egg is enormous. Luckily, mother ostriches, who have to lay them, are pretty big, too. When Olga the ostrich laid her very first egg she was justly proud. It was large. It was smooth. It looked exactly as an egg should do. Olga called round all her friends and relatives to show them how clever she'd been to lay it.

"When you've laid as many eggs as I have," sighed her mother, "you won't be so chipper. They're a tie, eggs. You can't go out in the evening and leave them by themselves in case they get cold. They need watching all the time. And, of course, when they hatch it's even worse. Then your life's not your own. Still, it *is* a nice egg. I'm looking forward to being a granny at last."

Many of Olga's friends were equally unimpressed.

"Doesn't it *do* anything?" asked Simon, giving the egg an experimental kick. Olga stared at him coldly.

"You didn't do anything when you were in an egg, Simon," she said. "To be frank you don't do very much now. And please don't kick my egg."

Olga was looking forward to motherhood, on the whole. Life on the wide savannah was all very well, but there wasn't a lot to do. You could kick dust. You could run about a bit and worry a wildebeest. You could sit down

on the ground and pretend to be asleep (and keep one eye open for lions). But that was it, really. Olga thought it would be fun to teach a young ostrich all he or she needed to know. And when her youngster was old enough not to need her any more, she could lay another egg and start again.

Time seemed to pass very slowly on the savannah. Olga had begun to worry that all was not well with her egg, when one day she heard a little tapping sound and a crack appeared in the egg.

Olga watched eagerly as first a little orange beak and then a damp little head poked out of the egg, took a look around, and promptly popped back inside again.

Olga was a little startled. This wasn't supposed to happen, surely? She waited for a minute or two, but there was no more activity from the egg. Olga decided that it was time to intervene.

"Hello in there!" she called, looking down into the open egg.

"Go away!" said a little voice.

"But darling, it's your mummy here!" cooed Olga in her best maternal tones. "I'm so looking forward to getting to know you."

"No!" called the voice, and it sounded crosser than a dear little baby of any species had any right to be.

"You can't stay in there!" Olga tried to sound encouraging. "There is so much for you to do out here! It's lovely! Come and see!"

Even as she said these words, Olga felt a pang of conscience. As she gazed across the dusty plain, it was hard to summon up much enthusiasm for it. She understood completely when the little creature said from within the egg, "It isn't lovely. I had a look. It's dusty and boring. I'd rather stay here."

"You can't stay there," Olga said gently. "You need to eat, little one, and there is no more food for you in the egg. Come on. It will be okay. Really."

The baby ostrich was stubborn, but he wasn't stupid. He poked his head cautiously out of the egg again, looked around, shuddered, sighed, and slowly clambered out, shaking his skinny little legs.

Olga's heart filled with pride. Something about the little ostrich's jerky movements gave her an idea.

"I'm going to call you Jiggles," she said. "Is that okay?"

Jiggles jiggled.

"It's not bad," he said. "Where is everyone? It's not just you and me, is it?"

"No, we've got lots of friends and relatives," said Olga, "and, of course, your dad would love to be here but he bumped his beak trying to chase a Land Rover and has been taken to the animal hospital until he gets better. He'll be back before long, I expect. He's a bit accident prone. He once broke his leg kicking a warthog (they're a lot more solid than giraffes) and he lost a lot of feathers that time he tangled with a porcupine. But you'll like him when he comes back."

"What is there to eat, then?" asked Jiggles, looking with disfavour at the dusty ground and the few sparse trees on the horizon.

"Seeds," replied his mother, "leaves, fruit if you can find it, shoots if they come up, flowers if it rains, and insects if you can catch them."

"It's not what you would call a gourmet selection, is it?" commented Jiggles, scratching in the dust as a little ant ran by. "But, hmmm, ants aren't bad."

Over the next few days, Olga showed her youngster off to everyone she

met, and even they were impressed by
Jiggles' bright little eyes, sharp little
tongue and fast little legs. He could run
like the wind, soon leaving poor old Olga
gasping as she trotted after him.

It was late one evening, as the sun
set, red and round, over the savannah, that
Jiggles asked the question that Olga was
to come to dread over the months that
followed that evening.

"When do I learn to fly" asked the
young ostrich. "I reckon I'm ready, but I
don't know what to do."

"That's because you can't. Fly, I mean," said Olga.

"Can't? Why not?"

"Ostriches don't. Other birds fly, Jiggles. But ostriches simply don't. Maybe we did once, but not for thousands and thousands of years, I think. None of us flies. Honestly. You ask anyone."

Jiggles had a look of deep disbelief on his face. Over the next few weeks, he did ask anyone. In fact, he asked everyone, including an astonished leopard who was so stunned to be being asked a question by someone who looked like breakfast that he didn't even try to catch Jiggles.

Jiggles soon found that everyone was in agreement.

"Vultures fly," yawned a lion cub, "and parrots and flamingos. But ostriches don't. I'm very glad, myself."

"Why?" asked a startled Jiggles.

"Because of accidents," said the lion cub. "Think how dangerous it would be if something as big as an ostrich suddenly fell on you out of the sky. You wouldn't stand a chance."

"It wouldn't be all that great for the ostrich, either," said Jiggles coldly. "It doesn't seem to me that it's a good enough reason not even to try."

So Jiggles tried. He reasoned that ostriches must have wings for some reason. He ran along the ground, flapping as hard as he could, and frightened a number of gazelles into moving home, but he didn't leave the ground.

Next, Jiggles tried jumping off anthills. The ants didn't like it, but Jiggles didn't care. Over and over again, his large feet clambered up the anthill. Over and over again, his even larger body fell with a thud on the ground the other side.

In the end, an elderly elephant, who had an even larger body, came to have a word with young Jiggles, who was now almost as big as his mother and whose feathers were gradually becoming shiny black and white.

"Jiggles," he said, "give it a rest, can't you? You're making the ground shake so much I can't tell when my ghastly sister is about to arrive. I like to have enough to time to disappear under the mud in the waterhole. Three times last week she crept up and caught me because you were making so much noise jumping off that anthill. What are you trying to achieve, lad?"

Jiggles explained. The elephant looked pained.

"Give it up, Jiggles," he said, "and give it up now. You are an ostrich and you will never leave the ground for as long as you live. Your father will be home soon. Ask him about it. He's tried most silly things in his time, but even he never tried to fly, I think."

Jiggles tried to look respectful. The elephant was *very* big. But the ostrich just couldn't believe he was being as silly as all that. He always came back to the same question. Why did he have wings if he wasn't meant to fly?

It was a week or so later that a film crew arrived on the savannah. Several of the animals were given starring roles in the movie that was being made. A senior lion even had a speaking (well, roaring) part. Much to his disgust, Jiggles was not needed. Apparently there were to be no ostriches at all in the film. Indeed, an annoying man with a handkerchief wrapped around his head kept coming along and telling the ostriches not to drop feathers all over the place, as it spoilt the look of things.

Jiggles was strongly tempted to kick the annoying man, but his mother dragged him away, saying, "It's that sort of behaviour that always gets your father into trouble. I expect better of you, young Jiggles!"

After that, the frustrated ostrich tried to ignore the film people, but it wasn't easy, especially when they erected a huge tower right in the middle of the plain. At the top of it, an intrepid cameraman was filming the backs of a herd of gazelles passing underneath.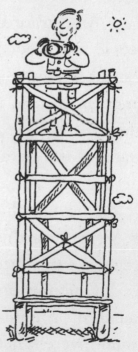

Gazelles are not the most intelligent creatures, and the shot had to be done time and time again. Meanwhile, Jiggles had suddenly seen the possibilities of the tower. If a fit and courageous bird (*with* wings) were to jump from the top, surely he would be high enough to start to fly? Jiggles made his plans.

An extraordinarily large number of people are needed to make a movie. It seemed to Jiggles as if there was someone or other around the tower all the time. Even at night, technicians were at work resetting the lights and checking scripts for the next day. It seemed that there would be no chance for Jiggles to get anywhere near the tower. But the ostrich, for once, was saved by the weather.

One morning, Jiggles awoke to the sound of coughing. Animals for miles around were wheezing and snorting as a duststorm swept over the plain. The movie crew were all hiding in their tents and trailers. Jiggles screwed up his eyes against the swirling dust and set off for the tower. His time had come.

It is very hard to climb ladders in a duststorm. It is almost impossible if you are an ostrich. The rungs are not made for big ostrich feet. The handrails are not designed for big ostrich wings. Above all, nothing human is meant to accommodate an ostrich's enormously long neck. Poor Jiggles really struggled as he made his perilous ascent.

Then, just as he neared the platform at the top, the duststorm suddenly settled as soon as it had begun. Jiggles looked out over the clear, sunlit savannah. It was perfect flying weather.

Of course, several animals and even more humans were looking out over the savannah as well. One of them happened to look up. There soon was not a living creature within twenty miles who did not know that a large ostrich was standing at the top of the scaffolding tower, preparing to jump.

Anxious relatives gathered around. "Don't jump, Jiggles!" they cried.

Anxious moviemakers huddled in groups, trying to think of a sensible way to move a fully grown ostrich (for Jiggles

was almost grown-up now) from eighty feet up in the air.

Jiggles flapped his wings. He took a step nearer the edge. He decided to count to five.

One...

Two...

Three...

Four...

"Don't do it, son!" yelled a powerful voice that Jiggles had never heard before. It was his father!

Jiggles hesitated, and as he did so, his dad opened his wings wide and *charged* at the crowd at the foot of the tower. He made a terrifying sight. Animals, humans and quite a lot of dust scattered as he approached. He didn't, however, quite manage to stop before he reached the tower.

Boing!!!

As his father's newly mended beak came into sharp contact with the steel poles that formed the tower, Jiggles jiggled dangerously. Swaying over the ground far, far below, jumping suddenly didn't seem such a wonderful idea. Jiggles clung with all his might to the platform, until it stopped rocking. Then, while his father kept back the crowds below, he climbed slowly down the ladder.

Jiggles and his father had a lot of catching up to do, but first the older ostrich had a few words to say on the subject of wings and their uses.

"Run at anyone or anything with your wings out wide," said Jiggles' dad, "and they'll back down. It's brilliant. Better than flying any day. It's what wings are for, lad."

Jiggles was impressed.

"Anyone or anything?" he queried.

His dad had the grace to look a little embarrassed.

"Except Land Rovers," confessed the ostrich. "And I'd give warthogs and porcupines a wide berth, too, but that's just a personal thing. I'm glad to know you, son!"

Mrs. Norton's Knitting

Some people collect stamps, or spot trains, or build model aircraft. There are those who paint horrible pictures and give them to all their friends. Most of us have a hobby of some kind, but Mrs. Norton's knitting was in a different class.

Mrs. Norton knitted from the moment she woke up in the morning to the moment her head touched the pillow at night. There were even rumours that she knitted in her sleep, but that was never proved. Ever since Mr. Norton had passed away ten years earlier, Mrs. Norton had lived alone with several thousand balls of wool and an array of knitting needles that looked like some kind of medieval torture machine when displayed together.

Now Mrs. Norton was a very enthusiastic knitter. She was a very quick knitter. But she wasn't a very *good* knitter. Her blankets usually had holes in them, and few people were persuaded by Mrs. Norton's protestations that they were part of a lacy pattern. Mrs. Norton's jumpers were no better. There was always one sleeve longer than the other, and neck holes were either so small that no one could pull them on or so loose that

wearers had been known to fall out of their sweaters as they walked along.

Mrs. Norton wasn't very good at choosing colours either. Her favourite combination was a deep cerise pink with lime green. She was quite fond of lilac and egg-yolk yellow, too. Best of all, Mrs. Norton liked to knit stripes. They were easy (although they still seemed to go wonky somehow) and they meant she could use all the different shades of wool she liked. Since Mrs. Norton even knitted in the dark if there was a power cut, she sometimes used shades she didn't like as well. But she could never, ever be accused of being tasteful.

Now, Mrs. Norton wasn't a great knitter but she was generous. She gave jumpers to all her friends. It was terribly easy to spot a Norton Knit from a hundred yards away. The stripes in horrible colours were a clue. The uneven arms and the neck problem only confirmed it. Mrs. Norton's neighbours didn't want to offend her. They tried to wear one of her jumpers once a year or so and make sure that she saw them. They tried to make sure that their other friends *didn't* see them!

A person only needs so many ugly striped sweaters. When she had knitted six sweaters each for everyone she knew, Mrs. Norton turned her needles to other

projects. She tried socks first, but it is terribly difficult to knit socks. They have heels that are tricky and toes that are testing. Mrs. Norton failed at every turn. She tried to pass off her efforts as leg-warmers for sheep, but the local farmers politely turned down her kind offers of free supplies. In the end, Mrs. Norton put away the socks in a deep cupboard and tried something else.

You might think that someone who has tried and failed to knit a decent sock would have more sense than to turn next to knitting gloves, but that is exactly what Mrs. Norton did. She was unbelievably hopeless. Her gloves never had the right numbers of fingers in the right places. Some of them would have been suitable for octopuses. Others would have made better socks than poor Mrs. Norton's intentional socks, if you see what I mean.

Mrs. Norton liked a challenge, but she had to confess that gloves had her beaten. Surely, she thought, there must be something simpler in her favourite book: *One Thousand Fascinating Projects for Knitters with Nerve*.

There was. Over the next few weeks, Mrs. Norton's nearest and dearest each received two dozen egg-cosies, fifteen bobble-hats, a charming cover for their toilet paper in the shape of a giraffe in a

waistcoat, and some knitted underpants. If you think about it, few things are less appealing than knitted underpants, and several of Mrs. Norton's neighbours took this as a sign that it was time they tried to wean her from knitting and find her another hobby.

It was an effort that was doomed before it began. Mrs. Norton never put down her knitting for long enough to *listen* to another idea, let alone to try it out. She would stare vaguely at her companion and say, "Sorry, what was that? I came to a complicated bit just then and couldn't concentrate on what you were saying."

Then the local vicar had a brilliant idea. It seemed that refugees in a cold country would be only too glad of any knitted items—even, he dared to suggest, handing back the pairs that Mrs. Norton had thoughtfully decorated with a cross—knitted underpants.

Mrs. Norton was very happy to hear that there was another outlet for her talents. She felt sorry for the freezing refugees and tried to knit faster than ever. Unfortunately, faster knitting meant more mistakes. Knitted underpants really shouldn't have more than two legs. Knitted hats should not be as big as buckets. Mrs. Norton felt sure they would prove useful for *something*, but she wasn't sure what.

The vicar had a large barn next to his vicarage where village fêtes were held if it was wet. Despite torrential rain the following summer, the vicar seemed strangely reluctant to open his barn and usher the merrymakers inside. Of course, he knew, as the others did not, that several bales of knitting, rejected even by the freezing refugees, were to be found inside. He simply could not bear to hurt Mrs. Norton's feelings by showing her how her handiwork had been received.

Now Mrs. Norton was such a demon knitter that she didn't put her needles down long enough to do any of the ordinary things of life. She didn't, for example, cook herself proper meals, but snacked on biscuits and crisps between rows. She didn't get as much sleep as she should either, as she always wanted to get just one more section finished before bed.

This meant that she was very often knitting into the early hours. Naturally, Mrs. Norton had no time for check-ups at the doctor's or healthy walks or changes of scene.

So perhaps it wasn't very surprising that Mrs. Norton became very ill. She had ignored the signs for years, and when she finally collapsed in a tangle of wool on her kitchen floor, she had to be rushed to hospital at once.

Luckily, a proper diet, rest and peace and quiet were all that Mrs. Norton needed. The doctor at the hospital was strict. No work of any kind. Gentle exercise. Good food. Lots of visits to friends and relatives. That was the recipe for Mrs. Norton.

Mrs. Norton felt like a car without wheels. It seemed so strange to have nothing at all to do with her hands. When she got home, she found that kind friends had removed every last scrap of wool and even her tiniest needles. She was so desperate, she even wondered if she could knit with wooden spoons and string, but she found that these had been taken away as well! Mrs. Norton sat in her house and felt very unhappy. In fact, she felt just the way she would have after her husband died if she had not had her knitting to keep her occupied.

As Mrs. Norton struggled with her feelings, the vicar was struggling with his barn door. As all Mrs. Norton's knitting equipment, plus the refugees' returned garments, plus several hundred knitted items that villagers had kindly given him (and each one bearing the unmistakable mark of Mrs. Norton's skills) were stored in his barn, he could hardly shut the door.

Now that she was no longer knitting, Mrs. Norton had time to do the normal things that most of us do. She read the paper and magazines. She watched television and listened to the radio. She found out, in other words, just exactly what was going on in the world outside—far from weird woollies and odd egg-cosies. She was amazed.

"Did you know," Mrs. Norton asked her neighbour over the fence onc morning, "that navy blue is *the* colour for mascara this year?"

The neighbour was stunned.

"Mascara?" she queried. "Do you mean merino, or perhaps mohair?"

"What? Those are kinds of wool!" cried Mrs. Norton. "You couldn't wear those on your eyelashes! Are you feeling quite well, dear? You should take it a little easier, like me."

When the vicar came to call, Mrs. Norton was eager to see him.

"I want you to try this spaghetti recipe," she cried. "I haven't done much cooking in recent years, so it will need a bit of fine tuning, but it tastes good."

The visitor was presented with something that looked suspiciously like some of Mrs. Norton's knitting, especially when he tried to wrap it around his fork.

It did, however, as she said, taste pretty good, especially coming from a cook who had not picked up a pan for ages.

Over the next few weeks, Mrs. Norton devoured daytime television and magazines of all kinds. She had a go at everything from model railway building (not a huge success) to cake decorating (interesting if you like modern art or are a fan of the way that building sites look after a demolition team has been in).

When she wasn't up to her elbows in glue or frosting, Mrs. Norton made some alarming experiments with make-up, and revealed that her colour sense for this was very similar to the skill she showed in choosing shades for knitting.

Mrs. Norton's cooking also became more adventurous. She delighted her friends and relatives with exotic dishes from around the world. Very few were identifiable on the plate, and Mrs. Norton's vagueness didn't help.

"Well," she would say, looking hopefully at a green and orange mixture lying like a cow pat in the middle of her plate, "this might be orange and pistachio mousse. On the other hand, it could be pea and squash medley. I can't remember what I tried in the end."

Tasting often revealed that Mrs. Norton's changes of heart occurred somewhere in the *middle* of a recipe, so

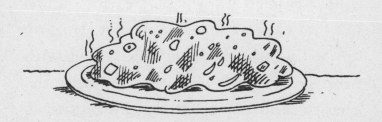

that visitors found themselves eating, say, orange and pea surprise.

One day, when Mrs. Norton was rushing through the village on her way to buy equipment for corn-dolly making, she met her friend Mrs. Stevens. Mrs. Norton looked with distress at the jumper her friend was wearing.

"Is business bad?" she asked with great sympathy. "Are you shopping in the charity shops, now? And if I may say so, my dear, purple and green with red stripes are not particularly good colours for you, not with an olive skin tone."

Mrs. Stevens was astonished.

"But Marla, my dear," she cried, "you knitted me this ... er ... *beautiful* jumper yourself last winter. Don't you remember?"

Mrs. Norton firmly denied all knowledge of the offending article, but as she walked back to her cottage, she did begin to remember. And as she walked, her face became pinker and pinker. She recalled now that quite a lot of mis-shapen articles had left her needles. Strangely, with so many new interests, she felt no need to take up knitting again, but she did feel a little embarrassed about the amount of knitwear with which she had showered her poor friends. Mrs. Norton was thinking so hard about this that she walked right into the vicar, who had been on his way to see her.

"Well, this is lucky," said the vicar, as he picked himself up off the road. "How are you, my dear Mrs. Norton?"

"As a matter of fact," replied the lady, "I'm feeling rather bad about something, but I don't know what to do about it."

"Something you've done?" asked the vicar. "Or something you haven't done, my dear?"

"Oh, something I've done!" cried Mrs. Norton. "Lots and lots of things I've done! I just don't know what to do to put things right."

"An apology?" suggested the vicar gently. "It can work wonders. Maybe if you told me what is troubling you…"

Mrs. Norton told him.

The vicar hesitated. Should he risk it? Then he told her about his barn full of knitted goods.

"If you can help me to find a home for them," he said, "I think we can call the whole chapter closed, Mrs. Norton. It is so good to see you looking happier again."

Mrs. Norton didn't hesitate.

"Recycling!" she cried. "I've been reading a lot about it recently."

The vicar looked dubious. "But I'm not sure anyone would want to wear…"

"No, no!" cried his parishioner. "It's the fibres that can be used, not the garments themselves (not that you can call most of them *garments*, I'm afraid). They can be used to make felt or stuff cushions and all sorts of things. I'll find an address for you."

Mrs. Norton was right. Not only was a company happy to come and take the awful objects off the vicar's hands, they even paid him money.

"The village fête will be better than ever this year!" he smiled. "And it's all down to you, Mrs. Norton. What would we do without you?"

Mrs. Norton blushed. "Perhaps you would like one of my handmade lampshades for the tombola," she said.

The vicar groaned. The knitting problem was solved, but there were so *many* crafts left!